MY FAKE SEA

MAIJA BARNETT

An imprint of Enslow Publishing
WEST 44 BOOKS™

Please visit our website, www.west44books.com.
For a free color catalog of all our high-quality books, call toll free 1-800-398-2504.

Cataloging-in-Publication Data
Names: Barnett, Maija.
Title: My fake sea / Maija Barnett.
Description: Buffalo, NY : West 44, 2027. | Series: West 44 MG verse
Identifiers: ISBN 9781978598683 (pbk.) | ISBN 9781978598676 (library bound) | ISBN 9781978598690 (ebook)
Subjects: LCSH: Champlain, Lake--Juvenile fiction. | Mermaids--Juvenile fiction. | Friendship--Juvenile fiction.
Classification: LCC PZ7.1.B376 My 2027 | DDC [F]--dc23

First Edition

Published in 2027 by
Enslow Publishing
2544 Clinton Street
Buffalo, NY 14224

Editor: Caitie McAneney
Designer: Tanya Dellaccio Keeney

Photo Credits: Cover (mermaid tails) oceanoart/Shutterstock.com; cover (Lake Champlain outline) Rumi designs/Shutterstock.com.

Printed in the United States of America

CPSIA compliance information: Batch #CS27W44: For further information contact Enslow Publishing LLC at 1-800-398-2504.

For Calista and Lyla-
may your lives be filled with wonder and magic.

"HEY, FISH EYES!"

I ignore
his voice.

Sharp
and grating
and very
            mean.

I wish
Brad Aster
would leave me
alone.

But he can't.
Or he won't.

I don't know
which.

I stare at the back
of the seat
in front of me.

While
the school bus
c r e a k s
to a joyless stop.
More kids
climb on.

But I don't
look.

I just lock my gaze
on the vinyl
seating.
Its color is like
my favorite seagrass.
Deep and mossy
with a hint of
sheen.

I pretend I'm there,
in the water.

And awful Brad Aster
with his nasty
grin
is someone
I don't even
know.

ME

My name is
Holly.

Holly
Smith.

A plain name
for a plain girl,
some might say.

Only anyone who said that
would be
wrong.

Because I'm not plain
in any sense of the word.

And I'm more magical
than anybody
you
know.

HOW I LOOK

I'm four foot eight,
with a bony
frame.

My fingers are
long and elegant,
but no one
ever
notices.

I have blue-black hair
that slides
down my back.

It reminds me of an
armload
of seaweed—

thick and
rubbery
and slick
with salt.

My skin is the color of
moonlit sand.

(Well, someone less creative
might say it's gray.)

But it's my eyes
that make people
look away.

They're pale and round
and very large.

I hide them behind
thick,
tinted glasses.

(On land, bright sunlight
makes it hard
to see.)

But everything's clear
underwater.

Down there, I'm not even
a little bit
strange.

SEVENTH GRADE MATH

Remember to blink,
I tell myself.

Blink.

Blink.

I hope someone
saw!

Sometimes when I'm
hyperfocused,
I forget to try and
not look
weird.

"So *x* stands for
a number,"
says Mr. Hinkle.

He squints at our class,
hoping we understand.

"If 2*x* equals 12,"
Mr. Hinkle continues . . .

“Then *x* equals 6,”
I respond.

I say the answer
under my breath.

But I’m in front,
so, of course, he hears.

Mr. Hinkle
smiles.

Runs a hand through his
thinning hair.

Then stares out at the
rest of the class.

I love
Mr. Hinkle.

And I love
math.

There’s safety in finding
the perfect solution.

In the real world,
x usually stays
unknown.

MY FAKE SEA

You'd think merfolk like us
would live near the ocean.

Well, most do.
But not Mom and me.

Mom's a free thinker.
(Or so she says.)

So we don't live
off the coast of Bali.
Or up in frozen Maine.

We live beside
a fake sea.

Lake Champlain was once part of
the Atlantic Ocean.

Salt waves kissed
its rocky shores.

But now it's trapped between
two mountain ranges.

I suppose it's landlocked,
just like me.

CLEAR WATER MER

is the organization
          Mom lives for.

She runs the
Lake Champlain chapter.
And she's all about
keeping
the lake water clean.

That and stopping
the sea lamprey
from devouring
too many fish.

SALT WATER AND SCIENCE

There's a mystery about the lake's
lamprey population.

One that Mom is trying
to solve.

You see, Champlain's lampreys
originally
came from the ocean.

Mom thinks that when the lake was
cut off,
they were trapped inside.

There, they evolved
for fresh water only.

Now, Mom wants to change that.
And return them to the sea.

She's experimenting with a
mermaid blood enzyme.

One that will allow the lampreys
to survive
in salt water again.

(Mom knows that
mermaids can breathe in
all types of water.
So there might be something
in our blood
that can help lampreys
do the same.)

She keeps an aquarium
in our basement.

Right now,
four tiny lampreys
are captive there.

(Which doesn't make Mom
much different
than the scientists we fear.)

Next to the tank sits Mom's centrifuge.
As well as vials
of her own blood.

So far, Mom's been
unsuccessful.

But I know Mom.
She *never*
          gives in.

SOLO

Mom works hard
to heal the lake.

But she doesn't work hard at
helping me.

I'm the only teen mermaid
in these parts.

(Like all of our kind,
my dad was human.
But he and Mom
didn't stay in touch.)

So, besides Mom,
I'm alone.
(Not that I haven't
tried making friends.)

But the kids here won't accept me.
And it's not just my looks.

It's because I keep
too many secrets.

But I can't let just
anyone in.

REASONS

There are two reasons
I want to join
Mom's organization.

First, I care
about the lake.

But, more importantly,
I *love* Rowen Wade.

Rowen is Mom's boss,
and a mermaid too.

She's smart and cool
and knows tons of
mermaid lore.

Rowen runs Clear Water Mer's
Maine chapter.

Mom's known her
since before
          I was born.

If Mom let me join
Clear Water Mer,
I'd get to work with Rowen too.
Plus, I'd finally have
somewhere
                    I belong.

(Then the shadows of sadness
would disappear.)

But Mom says
no.

Thirteen is
too young.

She thinks joining
will put me in
“risky situations.”

(And, unfortunately,
Rowen agrees.)

I know they’re right,
but it still hurts.

Especially since I’m stuck
keeping our secret
just by
being me.

FEARS

“Where are you going?” Mom asks
from our tattered sofa.
It’s adrift in lab work
and water quality charts.

It’s Saturday night,
and she’s studying
some papers.

They’re written in
Syreni,
which is fancy for
ancient Mer.

(Rowen taught me the letters.
But that’s
all I know.)

“Just swimming,” I answer.
Mom frowns.

“Stay away from
boats and beaches,”
she warns.

I sigh and say,
“I know the drill.”
Mom smiles,
but I sense
her worry.

It’s looming beneath her
too-pale skin
and glassy eyes
that look like mine.

I feel it
rising
in me too.

The fear of cameras

and scientists

and being trapped in
a tank.

Like the lampreys
Mom’s
experimenting on.

One mistake,
and that could
be me.

LATER THAT NIGHT . . .

I'm reading about
the U.S. Fish and Wildlife Service.
How they're poisoning lamprey larva
with lampricide.

Mom takes a call
from Clear Water Mer.

"You mean, someone's buying
Kyle Aster's land?"
She snaps into her phone.

"Agry Meats and Poultry?
The factory farm?
But, Rowen," shouts Mom.
"They'll pollute the lake!
They'll destroy the habitat."

Silence.
Mom groans.

I picture Brad Aster's family
losing their farm.

Then my insides
        twist.
I don't know why.

ARGUMENT

Next morning, Mom is
at the kitchen table,
staring into
          a cup of tea.

"Let me help save the Aster's farm,"
I say, plopping down
beside her.

"You overheard?" Mom asks,
surprised.

She shakes her long hair
that's the color of
pumpkins,
while I decide
what to say.

"I can be your assistant,"
I plead.
"I'll do the grunt work.
Come on, Mom.
                    Say yes!"

“Holly,” says Mom.
“You know I can’t let you.

Someday you’ll
understand.”

The look on Mom’s face
means her answer
is final.

I rush from the house,
toward
my fake sea.

ATTACK

It's sunny when I
enter
the water.

Mom hates when I do this,
but I don't care.

She'd prefer I go swimming
in total darkness.
Our secret hidden
          by the night.

I'm nearing the bottom
when something
latches
          onto me.

It's a giant lamprey,
and I can't get away!

I scream as its
circular rows of teeth
sink
into my tail.

Its sharp tongue
scrapes
my flesh and scales.

Now it's drinking my blood
like an underwater vampire.

Its three-foot-long body
is so slimy,
it's impossible to grab.

Another attaches,
and fear shoots through me.

Then a bright set of fins
appears in the deep.

Gloved hands rip the monsters
from me.

And guide me skyward,
toward the light.

"You okay?" asks the diver
once we've surfaced.

He yanks off his mask,
and my insides
freeze.

BULLY?

Brad Aster's face
is pinched.
His brown eyes wide.

My heart
clatters
against my ribcage

as I try to sink
beneath the waves.

But Brad is too fast.
He grabs my arm.

"You're a mermaid!" he cries,
gripping me tightly.
"I can't believe
you're actually real!"

For a moment, we're frozen,
both unsure what to do.

Then Brad's stare turns as deep
as the dark-gray water.
And I'm too injured
to swim
away.

CAUGHT

We cling to the side of
Brad's beat-up skiff.

Uncertain
of the other's
next move.

Then fear creeps
behind Brad's eyes.

And I wonder if he
regrets
saving me.

"I'm just me with a tail," I say,
the words rushing out.

Something shifts in Brad's gaze.
He shoves his dark curls
off his brow.

"Those things hurt you,"
he says, braver now.
"Do you want
a lift
to shore?"

STUCK

Part of me aches
to flee,
but why should I
bother?

Brad's already seen
what I am.

Yet, this is the boy
who teased me
for *years*.

Who acted like I was
infected with something.

Something he was
afraid
to catch.

Shivering,
I drag myself onto his skiff.
I hope I'm doing
the right
thing.

BRAD'S BOAT

It's about 10-feet long,
with a rusted-up
motor.

Its once-white
paint job
has started to molt.

I sit on a
cracked, wooden seat,
my scales
          gleaming.

The lampreys'
circular bite marks
trickle blood.

Brad hands me a towel,
and I wrap my tail in it.

Then a sickness
spreads through me
as I wait for
          the change.

SILENCE

Now, the world is
pulsing
around me.

The sky's
          bearing down.

The sun's a
          glittering eye.

But with my black wetsuit top
and my silver tail covered,
I look like a
          regular diver.

Not a mermaid
who's just been
          found out.

BRAD'S OFFER

It's Brad who
speaks first.

He's been fiddling with his
scuba tanks,
looking nervous and afraid.

"Holly,"
he says.

I stare at the water.
Because I really don't know
what to say.

"I have a proposition,"
says Brad,
dark eyes watching.

His build is lean.
You can tell he's a runner—
one of the fastest
in our grade.

"You might have wondered
why I was diving so deep,"
Brad continues.

Then he pulls a
damp wad of paper
from a backpack
near the bow.

As he unfolds it,
something inside me flutters.

“What’s that?” I ask.
“Are you searching for shipwrecks?”

Brad nods.
Then gives me the map.

It’s a hand-drawn outline
of Lake Champlain
with various X’s
marked throughout.

“There’s a wreck I need to find,”
says Brad.

“If you help,
I won’t tell
what you really are.”

"WHAT WRECK?"

I ask.

"It's called the *Sage*,"
Brad answers.
"And the treasure
it's carrying
could save my
family's farm."

"You mean, from
Agry's Meat and Poultry?" I say.

An image of
sick, mangy chickens
slides through my mind.
They're pecking and screeching.
There are too many
to count.

"How did you know?" asks Brad.
"Did my Uncle Charlie tell you?
Dad says Charlie's the reason
we're in this mess.
He and his
gambling problem, that is."

"My mom works for an
environmental group," I say.
"I overheard her talking.
That's all."

Brad drops his head
into his hands.

When he looks up,
his eyes are sad.

"I know you don't like me,"
he says.
"I mean, I haven't exactly been
nice."

"No, you haven't,"
I snap.

"Well, I've had my reasons,"
says Brad.

"To torture me?" I ask.

"I never tortured you," he replies.
"I was just kind of . . ."

". . . a jerk?" I say.

"Yeah," says Brad,
ears turning pink.

"Look, I'm sorry," he pleads.
"I really am.
But what do you say?
Will you help me
                    or not?"

"TELL ME ABOUT THE SHIP"

I say,
insides churning.

But no matter how hard I try,
I can't change
what happened.

I can't make it so Brad
doesn't know
what I am.

Which means,
I have no choice
but to help him.

Except, even if I do,
will he keep
          my secret?

Mom's face flashes
behind my eyes.

I see her red hair.
Her freckled hands.

Then Rowen's voice slides
through my mind.
And I remember
all they've done
to keep me safe.

Only, I've rolled the
protective ball of yarn
they've wound tightly
around me
directly off
the side of a cliff.

Unless I help Brad
find this ship.

Maybe that will make
everything right?

If we saved Brad's farm,
I would earn
Mom and Rowen's
          respect.

Then they'd have to let me
join
Clear Water Mer.

I might even earn
Brad's respect too.

I'll fix
both halves
of my broken world.
And I'll finally
                    belong.

A delicate calmness
blooms
inside me.
Like a flower
opening
to the sun.
I smile and stare at my
former bully.

Then I listen to what
he has to say.

HISTORY LESSON

"I'm looking for
Spanish escudos,"
says Brad.

"For *what*?"
I say.

"Gold coins,"
he replies.

"My Uncle Charlie's been
talking about the *Sage*
since I was little," Brad continues.

"It was a small sloop
owned by the
Continental Congress.

And it was sunk
by the British
during the Revolutionary War.

According to legend,
the ship went down
with a stash of
                    escudos.

They were loaned by the Spanish
to help the colonists
fight the British.

Throughout the years,
treasure hunters searched."
Brad continues.

"Now some claim
the *Sage*
is a myth.

But that can't
be true.

I mean, I've done
the research.

I *have* to find
the *Sage's* grave.

If I don't, our farm
is lost."

Brad's features twist
from excited to worried.

He glances at me,
and his eyes get bright.

"But now I've found you!"
he exclaims.

"And if mermaids are real,
maybe the *Sage* is too.

With your help,
I might actually find it!"

Brad's voice
cracks
when he says that.

He looks
          away.

I peer at the
sun-flecked water,
wondering what this
new alliance
          will bring.

"BUT WHY WON'T YOU TELL?"

I ask,
once we've reached
the dock.

Amazingly,
Brad's rickety boat
made it.

He falls silent
at my question.

My insides constrict
as I brace for
his response.

RESPONSE

"I know I've been mean,"
says Brad
once we've moored.
"But that's not
who I am."

"Then why were you
like that?" I ask.

"I was angry," he says.
"And you were
an easy mark.
It's not something
I'm proud of.
I want to
make it right."

"If I help you . . ." I say.
Brad sighs.

"Look, Holly," says Brad.
"I can't do this without you."

"Okay," I reply,
since I have no
choice.

PLAN

"Have you been to the
Lake Champlain Maritime Museum?"
I ask.

Unease brews inside me.
But I swallow it down.

"Of course," says Brad.
"That's where I found
most of my
dive sites."

"And the library?"
I say.

Brad rolls
his eyes.

"I've searched everywhere," says Brad.
"Not that it's done any good.
So far, I've come up
empty-handed."

"Let's go back to the museum,"
I say.
"Maybe we'll find
something new."
Brad smiles
like we're friends.

But his eyes
pierce my back
when I turn
          for home.

HOMEROOM

The next day, school is
a little strange.

I'm at my desk,
minding my own business,
when ultra-popular Erin Linto
tells me I have
          dead-fish eyes.

"Quit it, Erin,"
Brad hisses.

Then
          it starts.

Erin shakes her long, glossy hair.
Curls her lip.

Experience tells me
she's on the attack.

"New girlfriend, Brad?"
coos Erin,
voice scalpel sharp.

She knows what she's doing,
and so does everyone else.

Ms. Stevens
just stepped out of the room.

And no one dares
shut this down.

Not unless
they want to be next.

“Shut it!” Brad growls.
But we all see
he’s blushing.

It’s creeping up from his collar.
Spreading through
his cheeks.

“She is!” cackles Erin,
delighted.

Oh, how I want to
disappear.

I slink low in my seat.
Fake interest in my notebook.

“Don’t be embarrassed!” howls Erin.

The whole class
                    laughs.

MEETING

Brad and I meet
in the library
after school.
Make plans to visit
the maritime museum
in Vergennes.

“How will we get there?”
Brad asks.
“It’s an hour south.”

“My mom can take us,” I say.
“She’ll agree.”

Brad nods,
but I know
          something’s up.

It’s the way he taps his
worn-out sneakers.

How he won't look me
in the eye.

"Listen, Holly," says Brad,
still staring at his feet.
"I'm sorry about homeroom today."

"It's fine," I say.
"That stuff doesn't
bother me."

"Really?" says Brad.

I can tell he doesn't
buy my lie.

SATURDAY

The next day is Saturday,
and Mom agrees
to drive.

I guess nothing works better
than a mother's
guilt.

(I mean, Mom knows
I'm basically starved
for friends.)

I say I'm doing a project
on Lake Champlain's history.

And that my partner and I
need a lift to Vergennes.

"*You* have a partner?" gasps Mom,
wide-eyed.

Her smile
heats my skin
like the afternoon sun.

DRIVING WITH MOM

I'm in the front
passenger seat.
Brad sits
        right behind.

But I know
what he's doing.

He's studying
Mom.

Wondering if she's
a mermaid too.

After all, like me, she's wearing
tinted glasses.
When it's too gray
for a human
to need them at all.

"So, your father's in farming?"
Mom asks,
breaking the silence.

Brad nods, while I think:
*Keep your last name
to yourself!*

I try sending this message
telepathically.

But I highly doubt
it's working.

(I wish I had
that kind of magic.
According to Rowen,
some mer actually do!)

But maybe I do have
special powers
because Brad doesn't say
another word.

Which leaves Mom to
wonder
which farm belongs to
his family.

And whether he's
an Aster or not.

MR. HINKLE

My insides
hitch
when we enter
the museum.

(I sent Mom for a coffee
so we could research
on our own.)

Because who do we see
behind the front desk
but the one and only
Mr. Hinkle.

“No way,”
Brad whispers.
“He wasn’t here
last time!”

“Well, he is now,” I hiss.
Unsure what to do.

Mr. Hinkle beams
when he spots us.
Waves us over.

His glasses
gleam
in the light.

"You work here?" asks Brad.
I frown at his rudeness.

"You're a math teacher,"
Brad continues.
"Why are you in a
museum?"

"I enjoy math *and* history,"
says Mr. Hinkle.
His eyes sparkle,
just like during
class.

"Besides," Mr. Hinkle continues.
"Both my boys are in college.
I need
the cash."

Brad frowns,
and I know
he's recalling the story.

(It went around school
at the start of the year.)

How Mr. Hinkle's wife
died
in a terrible car wreck.

Leaving him
and his twin boys
alone.

I nudge Brad's foot
to signal
I'll do the talking.

Then I explain
why we've come.

I SPY

While I’m talking,
something
glistens
in the corner.

Past Mr. Hinkle’s desk
and a row of
tiny, bottled ships,
something magic
beckons me.

“I’ve studied every map here,”
complains Brad,
after I’ve finished
our story.

Mr. Hinkle nods,
says he’ll try and help.

“Holly?” says Brad.
He can tell I’ve stopped
paying attention.

I ignore him
and step toward the
strange light.

MAP

"*That* map?" says Brad.
"With the 'supposed' shipwrecks?

I checked it
already.

It didn't help!

I got most of my
dive sites
          from that thing.

None of them led
to the *Sage*."

MAGIC?

I stare at the
shiny blue symbol
stuck in the map's
righthand corner.

It's a semicircle,
about the size of a
penny.
And it's decorated
with
silvery scales.

The scales ripple,
like they're underwater.

I sense magic
waiting there.

"Hey, Mr. Hinkle," I call.
"Would you mind taking this
out of its frame?"

RESEARCH

We follow Mr. Hinkle to the
museum's basement
to get a special tool
for the frame.

It's dim and musty
and filled with
boxes and books.

Mr. Hinkle
opens
the wooden frame.

But when he slides out
the map,
something else
slips out
        too.

DISCOVERY

A sheet the size of my palm
flutters to the floor.

Brad grabs it,
and we see
it's another map.

I eye the miniature
curves of
Lake Champlain's shoreline.

The three
golden X's
marked inside
the lake.

The map's borders
are stained a
bluish purple.

Like it belongs
to the water,
not a museum.

Strange writing
encircles
the lake's outline.
If it's Syreni,
I can't make out
a word.

"Maybe one of those X's
marks the *Sage*,"
Brad whispers.

He whips out his
cell phone.

But Mr. Hinkle yells,
"No!"

"We have no idea
who hid this," warns Mr. Hinkle.
"I'd rather not have
your discovery
leaked onto the web."

COPIES AND CONCERNS

"Well, we *need* a photo,"
says Brad.

Mr. Hinkle
nods.

Then he leads us to an
ancient copier,
squat and dusty
in a corner
          of the room.

It takes Mr. Hinkle
a beat
to get it working.

But when we finally
head upstairs,
Brad's holding a copy of
our find.

"This better be it," he says.
"I need that treasure
if I want to save
          my family's farm."

The look in Mr. Hinkle's eyes
shows he knows
Brad's story.

There's sympathy there.
And sadness
too.

"You know,"
says Mr. Hinkle, softly.
"Anything you find
is the property of
whoever owns the lakebed.
So that's Vermont,
New York,
or Canada."

A lump forms in my throat.

"Of course," Mr. Hinkle continues,
"if a person really
needed the money,
he could take
some of the treasure.
No one
would know."

I stare at my teacher,
confused.
Is he saying
it's okay to steal?

"Secrets," scoffs Mr. Hinkle.
"Everybody has them."

Then he hangs the yellowing map
with the magical marking
back on
the museum's wall.

Our discovery's there too—
tucked behind the original.
As if no one had ever
found it
at all.

OUTSIDE, WAITING FOR MOM

"Those three X's," says Brad.
"I can't wait to dive them.
We just need to make
a pit stop first."

"A pit stop?"
I ask.

"I need air,"
says Brad.

I stare at him,
blankly.

"For my tanks."
He grins.
"We can't all
breathe underwater, like you."

"Where do you
fill them?" I ask.

"At my uncle's dive shop
in Plattsburgh," Brad replies.
"How do you feel about
ferry rides?"

TRIP TO PLATTSBURGH, NY

On Sunday,
we meet on Church Street.
Brad brings
his tanks.

He carries one,
hands me
the other.

Then we pick up a
rideshare
he's organized
to the ferry
to Plattsburgh.

"I'm paying," says Brad,
opening his wallet.

Inside, there's
a wad of cash.

"I took this from my dad
while he was sleeping,"
Brad tells me.
"He's sure gonna be mad
when he realizes it's gone."

DEEP DIVE

It's noon by the time
we get to
Deep Dive—

the specialty dive shop
Brad's uncle owns.

It's in a small, shabby storefront
near the docks.
And it's painted the color of
old snow.

My heart flutters
when we enter.

Because I know
I'm somewhere
I don't belong.

"Listen," Brad whispers.
"I'll do the talking.
Now, let's get this
over with."

UNCLE CHARLIE

Brad's uncle Charlie
is behind the counter.

I see the resemblance
right away.

Though he's stockier
than Brad,
he has the same
dark curls.

Except Brad's uncle's hair
is streaked with
gray.

Uncle Charlie looks up
when we enter,
and his blue eyes
soften.

I see sadness
in them too.

I'm pretending to check out
the wet suits
when Uncle Charlie
starts to speak.

"HEY, NEPHEW!"

"What can I do
for ya?"

Brad's uncle sounds
friendly.
But you never know.

"I need to fill these with
Trimix," says Brad.
He gestures to his tanks,
propped against
the wall.

Uncle Charlie raises
his eyebrows.
"So, you're diving deep, huh?
Well," he continues,
"as always, it's on the house!"

Then Uncle Charlie's gaze
shifts to me.

"You look familiar," he says.
"Aren't you
Laurel Smith's kid?"

"YOU KNOW MY MOM?"

I say.

"Sure do," says Uncle Charlie,
stepping from behind
the counter.
"I've done some work with
Clear Water.

But, as I'm sure
Brad's told you,
I'm a farmer at heart.

I only wish our farm
was doing more
to curb lake pollution."

Before I can respond,
Brad rolls his eyes.
Then he mutters,
"Like you care."

FILLING UP

"Brad," responds Charlie,
his voice steady
                    and kind.
"Why don't you help me
fill these up?"

Charlie shoots me a smile
and hoists up
one of the tanks.

Brad grunts and
grabs the other.

Then they disappear
out back.

RETURN

Brad stays silent
for most of the trip
                    back home.

We stand at the
ferry's bow,
watching the waves below.

It's only when we
near the shoreline
that he reveals
what's on his mind.

WHAT UNCLE CHARLIE SAID

"It's my dad who lost the farm,"
Brad tells me.

I can barely hear him
over the engine's roar.

"*He's* the gambler," says Brad,
blinking back tears.

"Are you sure your uncle's
being honest?" I ask.

Brad nods.
"Charlie showed me
the texts on his phone.
Guess that's why I found
all that cash
in Dad's wallet.

My own father's been
lying
all along."

BACK HOME

A dark-blue pickup
rests in our driveway.

“Rowen!” I squeal,
sprinting inside.

Rowen sits in the kitchen,
sipping tea.

“Baby Turtle!” she cries,
leaping up when she sees me.

Mom
cackles
          in delight.

I take in Rowen’s blond hair
and short, thick frame.

Her lipstick smile,
red and wide.

“Come here!” cries Rowen,
pulling me to her.

I inhale her scent
of salt and rain.

QUESTIONS

"Holly," says Rowen,
once we separate.

She brushes a strand of hair
from my face.

"Did I spot you at the
Grand Isle ferry today?"

Her voice always has
this singsong quality to it.

It reminds me of magic
and lullabies.

"No," I say,
my eyes darting
to Mom.

"Oh," laughs Rowen.
"My mistake!"

TAROT

After dinner,
Rowen breaks out
the Tarot cards.

She's been reading
my fortune
since I was small.

She's usually silly
when we do this.

But tonight,
her eyes are
          two dark seas.

"Pick three" says Rowen,
fanning out the deck.

For a moment, I'm nervous.
But I push the worry away.

Dishes clatter
as Mom cleans up
the kitchen.

"Ok," I say.
Then, I choose.

FORTUNE

Three cards lie
on the table
before me:

the Devil, the Moon,
and the Fool.

My world
freezes.

Then, Rowen
grabs my hand.

"A forbidden quest."
She smiles.
"How exciting!"

"Yeah," I reply,
trying to smile too.

MIDNIGHT TEXTS

Brad, u awake?

Yup

I just got a Tarot reading

???

You know, fortune telling stuff . . .

Yeah?

What did it say?

That I'm going on a forbidden quest
Are we set for tomorrow?
Do u have everything?

I've got rope, air tanks,
& my boat has gas

Now get some rest
Tomorrow's treasure hunting time! ☺

SATURDAY MORNING

Brad and I are at the dock,
loading gear.
I glance up
and notice
the bruised sky.

"Storm's brewing," says Brad.
"Funny, my weather app
didn't mention it.
Should we go
another day?"

"I wouldn't,"
calls a singsong voice
behind us.

When we turn,
we're confronted by
ice-blond hair.

And a magical stare
I've always loved.

"ROWEN?"

I say.

She clasps
my hand.

"Oh, Holly!" cries Rowen.
"I knew you were
up to something.
All I want to do
is help!"

"Wait, who are you?" asks Brad,
cutting in.

Worry flickers
across his face.

"It's fine," I tell him.
"Rowen's a family friend."

"Another mermaid?"
he whispers.

Behind her thick, tinted glasses,
Rowen's eyes
go wide.

HOW ROWEN KNEW

"How did you know
we were here?" asks Brad.

"Oh!" gasps Rowen,
warmly.
(Ignoring the fact
that Brad knows
what we are.)
"I was drawn by the
map's magic.
Holly activated it
when she discovered
where it was."

"Magic?"
asks Brad.

"You didn't tell him?"
gasps Rowen, turning to me.
"You didn't mention the symbol
on the map in the museum?"

"Holly?"
Brad's voice is measured.

But I still feel his anger—
dark as the sky.

OF COURSE

"The Syreni text
is asking to be read,"
Rowen said.

"Wait, you can read this?"
asks Brad,
waving the map
at Rowen.

"I'm a siren," replies Rowen.
"Of course I can!"

DEAL

"Hand me that map,
and I'll show you,"
says Rowen.
"But the deal is,
if I read it,
you'll let me
dive for the gold."

"What about Mom?" I warn.
"She won't like this."

"Oh, Holly," sighs Rowen.
"I've known your mother
since before you were born.
Sometimes
we just don't
agree.

Now, with my help,
I know you're
mature enough
to do this.

So give me the map.
Let's see what it says."

"YOU KNOW ABOUT THE GOLD?"

Brad asks.

"Of course!" replies Rowen.
"The decoy map's signal
filled me in."

"Wait . . . that map
sent you a message?" says Brad.
"Like a magical email?"

Rowen
        laughs.

"Then why doesn't Mom
know too?" I ask.

"Oh, your mother doesn't have
that kind of power," snaps Rowen.
"Why do you think
        I'm her boss?"

MAP READING

"Follow me,"
says Rowen.

Brad nods.

I bite my lip,
still worried
about Mom.

We follow Rowen
to her truck.

She snatches something
off the seat.

At first, it looks like
a clear sheet of plastic,
slightly larger than our map.

But when the light
hits it right,
it shivers.

That's how I know
it's alive.

"What *is* that?"
I ask.

"An overlay," says Rowen.
"Made from sea salps."

"Sea salps?" Brad repeats,
confused.

Rowen sighs and mutters,
"What *are* they teaching you
in school?"

Then she tells us that salps
are gooey invertebrates.
Like jellyfish,
          only smaller.

"These salps," continues Rowen,
"will give us answers."

Then she lays the
glistening salp sheet
over the map,
and its gibberish
twists into something real.

"It's Syreni!" I gasp.
Rowen grins.

"THERE'S THE *SAGE*,"

murmurs Rowen,
reading the name beneath
the center X.
"The wreck to the left
is the USS *Yellowjacket*.
And the one in the corner
is the HMS *Regal*."

"Wow! I can read it!" I say,
excitement coursing through me.

Brad stares
in awe.

"Are those decoy wrecks?"
he whispers.

Rowen nods.

"But what about the words
rimming the lake?" I ask.

I gaze at Rowen
in admiration.

"I'm bad at Syreni," I whisper.
"Rowen, what do they say?"

ROWEN READS

Dear Reader,
If you understand this message,
than you know
what I am.

For like you—
I am of
mer blood.

But I'm also
a curator
of history itself.

Presently, I'm a
maritime historian
stationed on Lake Champlain.

(This is not a role often given to
18th century women.
But the people here
fear me—
as they should.)

It's through my position
that I learned of
the Sage's wreck.

As well as the treasure
locked within.

You will find the ship marked
on this map.
Along with two decoy sites.

Now, I've hidden this map,
as a promise to our kind.

For within the
sleeping Sage
lies great wealth.

I've kept it
for our future.

For a mer
in need.

And if that is you,
dear sister,
then rejoice!

Warmly,

Dr. Elizabeth Grange

WEATHER SONG

"An 18th century mermaid
left this?" cries Brad.
"I can't believe there are
so many of you.
I always thought mermaids were
a myth!"

Rowen smiles
then starts to sing.

The song that curls out
reminds me of water.

Of the smell of
my mother.

Of salt on
my skin.

I peer at the sky
and notice
the clouds have parted.

"You can control
the weather?" I whisper.

Why didn't I know that?

DIVE SITE

We're at the dive site.

Rowen's staying aboard,
keeping the weather safe.

Worry pricks my insides,
but I ignore it.

Only, I can't stop wondering
why Rowen never mentioned
the weather thing.

When I asked,
she was too busy singing
to tell me.

DESCENT

Slowly,
we glide
into darkness.

Allowing time for
Brad's body
to adjust.

As our world
blackens,
we switch on
our flashlights.

We mermaids can see
in darker waters
than humans.

But my heart still craves
the safety
of the light.

120 FEET DOWN

That's when we
see it.

The ship
reaching
from the deep.

Fear quivers
through me.

I sense
death lurking.

I'm not sure I dare
go inside.

Then Brad grabs my arm
and points to the guide line.
It's carefully looped over his arm.

He unwinds it and ties one end
to a metal drum.
It sits, sentinel-like,
on the lake's silty floor.

ENTERING

Brad signals *okay*,
and we enter.

The *Sage's* walls
close in.

It takes a moment
to get our bearings.

Then we head for the
captain's quarters,
in the stern.

When we finally arrive,
the safe is missing.

I turn toward
a darkened corner,
and a brittle skeleton
grins back.

JUMP SCARE

I scream
into the
shadowed water.

Then Brad
grabs my hand.

He gives another
okay.

I guess this stuff
doesn't scare him.

Right, I think.
You better be brave too.

I swim forward,
toward the skeleton
captain.

Behind his
pale bones
sits a trunk full of gold!

TIME TO GO

Brad signals
something's wrong.

He points to his
regulator.

He's low
on air.

I open the small
diving bag
around my waist.

But before I can grab
a single escudo,
something darts
from the deep.

"No!" I scream,
as it latches onto me.

A cloud of
snakelike bodies
appears.

Then, there's Rowen—
pale hair gleaming.
My heart leaps
in relief.

Rowen opens her mouth.
And the song that comes out
sounds like
dolphins calling.

(It's how we mer
communicate
underwater.)

"Rowen!" I scream,
in my own dolphin cry.

She turns to me then,
and her face is wrong.

The love I usually see
is missing.

"Rowen?" I cry.
She doesn't respond.

But the lampreys do.
And they do her
bidding.

I shriek as they suction
onto my skin.

BETRAYED

"Rowen, help!"
I beg.

She turns
away.

The lampreys' sharp tongues
scrape
my scales.

"Rowen!" I howl.
"I don't understand!
Why are you
doing this?"

THIEF

Now Brad is
tearing
at the lampreys.

Only they're too slippery.
He can't
pull them off.

Then Rowen's voice
winds through the darkness.

She's still commanding
the lampreys.

And she won't
look at me.

I sob as she
swims
toward the treasure.

Is she trading my life
for gold?

DEATH BY LAMPREY?

The world is fading
around me.

Rowen finally
swims away.

There are too many
escudos
to steal at once.

She has to surface
and return.

Brad struggles to pry
off the lampreys.

My breathing's grown shallow.
I'm almost gone.

Without thinking,
I scream into the ocean.

I cry out
to the lampreys.

Somehow,
          they understand.

OH, SIREN

Sings a chorus of
serpentine voices.

(Only, they're not
actually speaking.
No, I can hear them
in my
          mind!)

Our mistress promised us
a mermaid for supper.
So confide what you wish.
Then we shall
                    feed.

I GASP

Tail flailing.

"You can hear me?

Are you *magical* lampreys?

What's going on?"

A FISHY DISCUSSION

The lampreys
detach
from my body.

Blood starts streaming
from my tail.

(And with it,
my strength.)
Brad shines his flashlight
on the lampreys.

Their long, fleshy bodies
shiver in the light.

"Why are you attacking me?"
I moan into the water.
"And why can we
communicate?"

The lampreys raise their heads,
and their words pass through me.

Like a current of meaning.
Meant for me, alone.

WHY THE LAMPREYS CAN SPEAK

You can hear us,
sing the lampreys,
because of what we've slipped
into your body.

The anticoagulant
in our saliva
thins your blood.

But when enough of it
enters
a mermaid's bloodstream,
it allows her
to hear us
            in her mind.

Rowen taught us
that trick.

She learned it
from our brothers.

It was how she was able
to communicate
            her plan.

ENEMIES?

Rowen sent us,
the lampreys continue.
For mermaid tail
is a lamprey treat.

She promised yours.
If we helped her.
So, we agreed.

You see, Rowen was injured
in the Atlantic.
Our salty brothers found her there.

On spying her tail,
they began to feed.

But once they learned she could hear them,
they released her.

Which we won't
be doing to you.

"Please," I beg,
trembling at their laughter.

Not unless, they hiss,
you have something to trade?

FIGHTING TERROR

Fear sears my insides.
It's hard to think.

Brad swims toward me.
I signal, *wait*.

I eye the eellike creatures
before me.

And I slowly come up
with a plan.

"Rowen tricked you," I murmur.
"She's giving you
nothing.
Just a quick snack
while she steals the gold."

We have no need
for money,
the lampreys hiss.

"But you do need freedom,"
I cry.

The lampreys
freeze.

PROBLEM SOLVING

We are free,
sing the lampreys.

"But not like you would be
in the ocean,"
        I counter.

I'm shaking with effort.
But I force myself on.

I try and recall
what I've learned about
Lake Champlain's lampreys.

Then my mind flashes
to Mom.
And the lampreys
in our basement.

Her bloody
vials.

Something starts to
click.

So far, the enzymes
Mom's fed them
haven't made enough of a difference.

Unless . . .

I wonder . . .

Did she not feed them enough?

It's like I'm solving for x
back in
Mr. Hinkle's math class.

Then the answer
appears
in my mind.

SPEECH

"I can save you," I sing
through the
          inky water.

The lampreys' snake heads
turn to me.

"I may have a way
to return you
to the ocean," I tell them.
"To a better, safer
home.
Away from this lake,
where you are
destroying
the ecosystem.
Devouring the fish population.
Consuming
it all.
While we hunt
you down
with traps and poisons.
Even murdering
your babies
before they have a chance
to grow.

"But if you trust me
to take you
to the ocean,
you'll find a world
where you
belong.

Humans won't hunt you
in those
salty waters.

And mermaids won't either.
You'll finally
be free."

BUT HOW?

Hiss the lampreys,
pale eyes gleaming.

I point
          to my tail.

"You just have to
feed."

COMPLETE ANSWER

"My mother is working on
an experiment,"
I tell the lampreys.

Their tails
flick, impatiently.

I go on.

"I think the part of my blood
that lets us
communicate
is the same part
that will allow you
to return
          to the sea.

You see, Mom keeps
a few of your kind
in an aquarium."

The lampreys glare
when I say that.

But I
can't stop now.

“Only, she’s never been able
to communicate
with them.

I think it’s because,
even though she feeds them
small vials
of mermaid-blood enzyme,

they don’t drink
enough
to make
          the change.”

THE LAMPREYS' DECISION

For a moment,
there's
            silence.

The lampreys
are communicating
in a way
I can't understand.

Suddenly, their bodies
start swaying.

I brace myself
for their final attack.

But instead of
swarming me,
they speak.

MAGIC BLOOD TRANSFER

Little mermaid,
hiss the lampreys, drawing closer.

We believe all you've
told us.

Your heart is pure.

And we feel
you are right.

Our kind is destroying
this lake
we live in.

So with your help,
we'd like to find
another home.

BLOOD SUCKERS

Then the lampreys' hiss
rises through the water.

They're calling their
brothers and sisters.

Telling them
to feed.

Soon, swarms of new lampreys
are sliding against me.

Their mouths clamp on.
They take
what they need.

I try not to
scream
as they drain
the blood from me.

While my skull vibrates
with their promise.

We won't overeat.
You will be
safe.

AFTERWARD

My tail feels like
fire
when the lampreys
finally finish.

Have they swallowed
too much?

Am I too weak
to swim?

Now Brad is dragging me
toward
          open water.

Suddenly, he turns,
hand slashing
at his throat.

It's the universal diving signal
for being
          out of air.

INDECISION

Brad's
drowning.

But I am frozen.

Deep-blue death
pulls me in.

Then the lampreys'
hiss
echoes through my body.

Save him, little sister! they sing.
You know what to do!

Their confidence in me
gives me strength.

NOT A KISS

We're still
80 feet down.

And Brad
is dying.

I tear off
his mask.
Press my lips
to his.

Slowly,
I guide us
through the water.

I force oxygen
into his lungs.

While making sure
we don't rise
too fast.

If we do,
the pressure change
could kill him.

It doesn't bother
mermaids.
But humans can't
tolerate it
at all.

Keep going,
I think,
swimming
skyward.

(Just like any other fish,
I must move to breathe.)

Below me stare the eyes
of a thousand lampreys.

Waiting to ensure
I don't drown.

WHAT?

When we finally surface,
Brad's boat
          is gone.

Rowen must have
taken it.

But she left something
in return.

She tied four orange
life jackets
to the emergency oars
that Brad keeps aboard,
just in case.

I pull Brad onto the
makeshift raft.

Then hope
he wakes up
soon.

WORRY

While I wait,
I try not to
think
          of Rowen.

Of how someone
I loved
could betray me
like that.

Instead, I focus on Brad,
praying his eyes
open.

Fear
burrows
through my heart.

SAVED

Just as I'm about to
lose hope, Brad twitches awake.

"You saved me,"
he croaks.

"Rowen stole your boat,"
I say.

Brad's face is pale.
"Well," he replies.
"At least we survived."

"You need a doctor,"
I tell him.

He shakes
          his head no.

"Get the treasure," he murmurs.
"I'll be
          okay."

INJURED

Then Brad sees
my tail,
all mottled and
bleeding.

“Never mind, Holly,”
he whispers.
“It’s not worth it
anymore.”

Something inside me
brightens
when he says that.

My bully—

the boy whose words
were torture—
is putting me
before
his family’s farm.

DECISION

"I can do it," I say.
"But Brad, while I'm gone,
you have a job too.
You need to figure out
how we're getting you
to safety."

"I don't know . . ." says Brad,
unsure.

"You'll think of something," I say,
slipping back
          into the water.

I disappear
before
he has a chance
to respond.

THERE

The *Sage*
looms
in the heavy
blackness.

I ignore my
throbbing tail.

Lock my fear
inside.

Without a flashlight,
the water is
dark and murky.

But I've found
Brad's guide line.

So I
            return.

TRAPPED

I'm at the
treasure now,
loading what's
left
          into my bag.

Then I hear Rowen
telling the lampreys
to charge.

My insides seize.
It's time to go.

But when I reach for
the guide line,
it's gone slack.

Rowen must have
cut the line!

"Stop her," commands Rowen.
There's movement in the water.

But instead of
attacking me,
the lampreys turn on Rowen.

THE LAMPREYS' CHOICE

Stay back, sea witch,
the lampreys hiss
in unison.

You have offered us
almost nothing.
While your sister will take us
somewhere new.

"New?"
cries Rowen.

Then I
          see her.

She's switched on
her flashlight.

I gasp
          in surprise.

A great wall of lampreys
floats between us
in the water.

And I'm on the side
with the gold.
"I can bring you
to the ocean!" cries Rowen,
desperately.
"I can give you her tail
and take you there."

The lampreys
stare,
eyes pale and knowing.

Rowen's fear
tangles
with my own.

No, siren, they hiss,
bodies
writhing.

We have already
chosen.

We've seen which of you
puts another's life
before her own.

We'll consume you
instead!

BETRAYAL

It takes
only a moment.
Then,
          they're on her.

Their sharp
angry mouths
dig into her arms
and tail.

"Help!" screams Rowen.
"Holly, please!
I did it for the good of
our kind!"

Her words vibrate
through the water.

And though part of me
longs to save her,
her betrayal
          keeps me away.

ROWEN'S PLAN

"Holly!" begs Rowen,
as the lampreys devour her.

"Our kind needs that treasure.
There's no other way!

The environment
is being poisoned.
And we can't
stop it!

I needed the gold
to keep our sisterhood safe.

I planned on purchasing
an island for mermaids.

Of course, we'd allow
some humans on it.
To keep our population strong.

But there, we mers
would be protected.

While we waited for the climate
to realign."

"BUT YOU WERE SACRIFICING ME!"

I cry,
my anger electric.
"I thought you
loved me!"

"I do,"
Rowen moans.
"But sometimes you must
give up what you love
for the greater good.
Even if it
            hurts."

Behind my eyes
race
memories of Rowen.

Like a movie
speeding
through my mind.

There's Rowen pushing
three-year-old me on the swings.

Rowen laughing and scattering
Tarot cards
on the floor.
I see Rowen's pale fingers
braiding my hair.

And the warmth of her hug
when we say
goodbye.

"STOP!"

I scream,
to the feeding lampreys.

Upon hearing my voice,
they freeze.

"Release her," I cry,
praying they listen.

Something in my heart
knows
they will.

For they aren't evil,
these snakelike creatures.
They just want to live
and let live.
Like all of us do.

LISTENING LAMPREYS

It takes only
a moment,
and Rowen is free.

Before she leaves,
I ask
about the raft.

Sobbing, Rowen glides
closer.

Her blond hair
rippling
in the watery dark.

"I didn't want to hurt you,"
she sobs.
"I made that raft
 in case you
 survived."

I know she's crying.
But the lake drinks her tears,
almost as if
they're nothing
 at all.

“Take your gold,” I tell her.
“Buy your island.

But I don’t want to
see you
ever again!”

Something inside me
breaks
when I say that.

As if my heart
is a crystal
shattering across
the floor.

GONE

Once Rowen is gone,
I haul the remaining gold
to the surface.

The lampreys disappear
to await my return.

Don't forget us, little mermaid,
they hiss.

"I've given you my promise,"
I reply.

As the ship
disappears
into the shadows,
I think about Rowen
and what she did.

She chose the safety
of our people
over a single mermaid.

Does it really matter
if that mermaid
                    was me?

HEADING HOME

"Holly!" Brad shouts
once I breach
the surface.

I slide the bag of
escudos
onto our makeshift raft.

The sun's bearing down,
brilliant and smiling.

And I know it's emerged
because Rowen is gone.

Brad's fixed the raft into
a sort of kayak.

He straddles the life preservers
while I steady
the loot.

Then, together, we start
the long trip home.

THREE-HOUR JOURNEY

My tail
screams
as I propel us
forward.

I keep checking on Brad.
Making sure he's okay.

He's trying to row.
But he's too weak
to do much.

(I guess that's what happens
when you almost
                    drown.)

I stare at the lake
stretched out before us.

And think of all I've lost
today.

Inside its depths
lies my love for Rowen.

Buried beneath
a sheet of gray.

MOM AND CHARLIE

When we finally arrive,
Mom and Charlie
are waiting.

I'm shocked to see them
when we float in.

My body burns
but I stay low
in the water.

So no one from shore
can see what I am.

"Holly!" shouts Mom,
signaling for me
to get on the dock.

Then she hugs me
and wraps my tail
in a towel.

"Charlie knows," she whispers,
holding me close.
"Rowen called us both.
Told us to hurry."

MOM THE PROTECTOR

Mom, Charlie, Brad, and I
sit around our
kitchen table.

Mom brewed a pot of tea,
and the hot liquid
seeps
into my bones.

"What should we do?"
asks Brad,
eyeing Mom, nervously.

"Well, I've alerted
Mer Headquarters," she says.
"So the search is on."

"The search?"
I say.

"They need to find Rowen,"
replies Mom.
"She almost killed you.
She'll have
to pay."

"But what about the fact
that she was
doing it to help us?" I ask.
"Not me, exactly,
but our kind?"

Mom's eyes fill with a mixture
of anger and
sadness.

"Her intentions don't matter,"
Mom hisses.
"And I will *never*
forgive her."

"WHAT ABOUT THE GOLD?"

Brad asks.

"You're keeping it,"
says Mom,
voice growing bright.

I know she's hurt
that Rowen
betrayed us.

But she's
future focused.

Which is what
I need.

"But Mr. Hinkle told us
we'd have to give it to
the authorities," says Brad.

"Well, we're not," Mom replies.
"We're giving it to you.
According to mermaid law,
the treasure is ours.
And we're using it to save
your family's farm.
Of course, there is one
condition," says Mom.

Brad and Charlie
nod.

"You need to make your farm
environmentally sound.
That means
no more pesticides
running into the lake.
And everything should be
organic.
We don't need any more
poison
destroying the land
and water."

"Deal!" shouts Charlie,
grinning.
"With the money we're getting,
we can make that work!"

AFTERMATH

Several weeks have passed
in a swirl of
water.

But life is richer
than before.

Once Mom learned what happened,
she ran to the basement.
Slipped both arms into
the aquarium.
Let the lampreys feed.

After they could communicate,
she apologized for her
experiment.

(They were more understanding,
than I thought they'd be.)

Then they asked her
not to release them
into Champlain's waters.

Instead, they wished to be
first
to greet the sea.

We gave the escudos
to Uncle Charlie.

He used his diving contacts
to sell them for cash.

Then Brad's family took the money
and repaid their debts.

I felt light
when I heard that.

Like things were finally
okay.

Like the terrible sadness
lurking inside me
had transformed into
gold.

WHAT HAPPENED TO THE FARM

Charlie sold his dive shop
so he could help run it.

And Brad's father joined
Gamblers Anonymous.
He's fighting his addiction
every day.

As for Agry's Meat and Poultry . . .
Well, they weren't happy.

After Mom told me that,
she let out a
whoop!

The sound of her
laughter
reminded me of
Brad's
air bubbles.

Perfect and gleaming and
rising toward the light.

GOODBYES

Every Sunday,
Brad, Uncle Charlie, and I
pile into Charlie's pickup.

We're at the Burlington docks
before sunrise.

Before even the fishermen
are awake.

I slide into the water
and call the lampreys.

(I hear them in my mind
before they arrive.)

I don't leave the lake
until I feed those who need it.

Then we drop them into
a saltwater tank
in the bed of Charlie's truck.

(The first time,
I was scared
the lampreys wouldn't make it.)

But the experiment worked.
They survived!

Hampton, New Hampshire,
is a three-hour drive.

We find a strip of empty coastline.
(A different spot each time.)

There, we release
the lampreys.

They thank me before
swimming free.

Sometimes, I hear them
in the darkness.

Their shadows hiss
as I melt toward sleep.

And sometimes I hear Rowen calling.
(Begging my forgiveness.
Which I finally give.)

I release her the way I do
the lampreys.

For in my heart,
I've set her free.

FRIENDS

School is different now.
I actually have friends.

And no.
I don't just mean Brad!

But Brad's popularity
helped.

Most people
are nice.

(Not Erin Linto.
I still avoid her.)

But I've become friends
with Dana Barns.

She's this red-haired girl
who sits behind me in math.

Yesterday, Dana said
she always thought I was cool.

She just wasn't sure
the right way
to say hi.

MR. HINKLE'S COMMENT

Today, Mr. Hinkle made
a comment
during math.

Something about
fish scales, and magic,
and heroes
in the night.

Though he doesn't know
everything,
Mom did give him
three escudos.

And Charlie promised to take him
to a historic dive site.

I know Mr. Hinkle
has his suspicions.

But I guess he was right
about people and secrets.

Because, so far,
he's kept things
to himself.

NOW

I suppose some secrets
should stay hidden
forever.

Especially the
magical kind.

They need to be kept
as transparent
as water.

Like a mermaid's tears
spreading
through the deep.

As the newest member
of Clear Water Mer,
I know this
to be true.

(And Brad and Uncle Charlie,
our honorary members,
agree.)

That's why I like to
explore
the Sage in private.
Shine my flashlight
on her lovely remains.

Down here, I'm
connected
to my true purpose.

I feel a sense of
belonging.
And a calmness too.

Day by day,
I'm finding myself
in these gray-green waters

as I work to protect
my fake sea.

Want to Keep Reading?

Here's a sneak peek at another book
from West 44 Books:

DAYLAN AND THE RIVER OF SECRETS
by Edd Tello

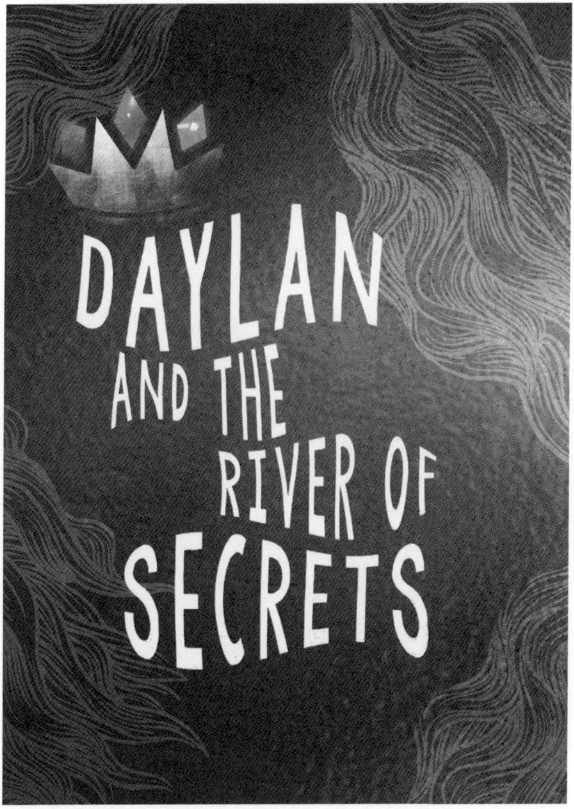

ISBN#: 9781978597488

SOMEDAY

I dip my toes into
the green-blue water.
Then my whole body
sinks.

I'm no longer
Scaredy Daylan.
I flutter kick.
My arms move in circles
in the cold river.
I float.

The warm rays of the sun
shine on my face.
I dive.

"Daylan Torres, it's five.
Time to go!"
I open my eyes.
I am still sitting on the stones.

Mamá hugs me from behind.
Her long straight hair falls on my
sweaty forehead.

Someday, I tell myself.
Someday, I will dive into the river again.

NEWBORNS

I put my life jacket and
goggles in the trunk.
Mom towel-dries her hair.

By the way she stares at me,
I know she's worried.
I know both she and Papá
would like me to swim again.
It's been three years.

In San José Lagos,
water is sacred.
We swim from the time we are born.
Parents put their babies
in the clean waters of
the Nacimiento River.

Nacimiento means "birth."
People here also
call the river *El Naci*.

I get into the car—
the same gray car
that Papá used to drive
before he left home.

CULEBRA

Dad left home
when I was nine.

For several months,
my parents' screams
were like a culebra
—a water snake.
They wound around my neck.

The fights happened more and more.
I felt as if a culebra
was dragging me
to the depths of El Naci.

One sunny afternoon,
Dad took me out
in this same car.

He said, sobbing,
"Sometimes relationships
don't work out.
You'll understand
when you grow up."

It's been three years,
and I still don't get it.

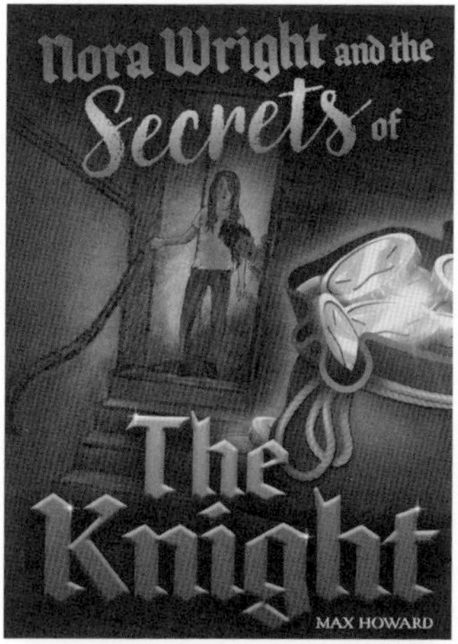
Nora Wright and the
Secrets of
The
Knight
MAX HOWARD

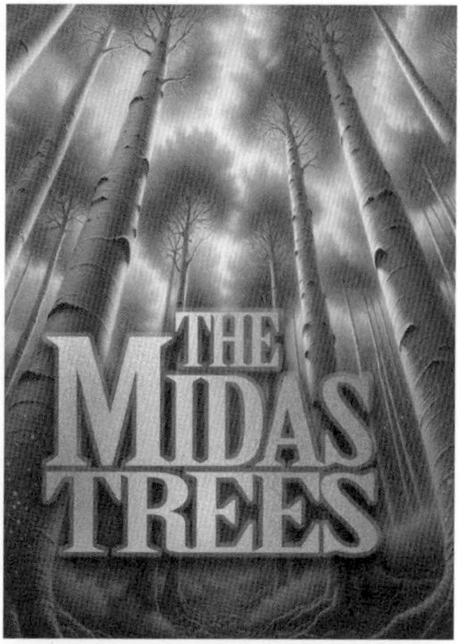
THE
MIDAS
TREES

LIAM AND
THE GIANT
EELS

STICKS
AND
STONES
ANN MALASPINA

ABOUT THE AUTHOR

Maija Barnett grew up in Vermont and now lives in Massachusetts with her family. She loves nature, poetry, hiking in the woods with her dogs, and finding ways to get kids excited about reading. Maija holds degrees in English and teaching and currently teaches at a school for students with learning differences. *My Fake Sea* is her sixth novel.